# BRAMBLEGOOP'S SIDEWAYS MAGIC

## When Fairies Go Too Far

written by
**KATE KORSH**

illustrated by
**MARTA ALTÉS**

putnam

G. P. Putnam's Sons

Look for all the
**Oona Bramblegoop's Sideways Magic**
books!

*Newbie Fairy*

*A Boy in the Fairy World*

*Fairies vs. Leprechauns*

*When Fairies Go Too Far*

❖ ❖ ❖

G. P. Putnam's Sons
An imprint of Penguin Random House LLC
1745 Broadway, New York, New York 10019

First published in the United States of America by G. P. Putnam's Sons,
an imprint of Penguin Random House LLC, 2025

Text copyright © 2025 by Kate Korsh | Illustrations copyright © 2025 by Marta Altés

Penguin Random House values and supports copyright. Copyright fuels creativity, encourages diverse voices, promotes free speech, and creates a vibrant culture. Thank you for buying an authorized edition of this book and for complying with copyright laws by not reproducing, scanning, or distributing any part of it in any form without permission. You are supporting writers and allowing Penguin Random House to continue to publish books for every reader. Please note that no part of this book may be used or reproduced in any manner for the purpose of training artificial intelligence technologies or systems.

G. P. Putnam's Sons is a registered trademark of Penguin Random House LLC.
The Penguin colophon is a registered trademark of Penguin Books Limited.

Visit us online at PenguinRandomHouse.com.

Library of Congress Cataloging-in-Publication Data
Names: Korsh, Kate, author. | Altés, Marta, illustrator.
Title: When fairies go too far / written by Kate Korsh; illustrated by Marta Altés.
Description: New York, New York: G. P. Putnam's Sons, 2025.
Series: Oona Bramblegoop's sideways magic; 4
Audience term: Children | Audience term: Preteens
Summary: As a newly appointed councilmember, Oona gets carried away creating new rules that unintentionally weaken the magic that hides the fairy world.
Identifiers: LCCN 2024034349 (print) | LCCN 2024034350 (ebook)
ISBN 9780593533727 (hardcover) | ISBN 9780593533734 (trade paperback)
ISBN 9780593533741 (epub)
Subjects: CYAC: Fairies—Fiction. | Magic—Fiction. | Fantasy. | LCGFT: Fantasy fiction.
Classification: LCC PZ7.1.K6816 Wh 2025 (print) | LCC PZ7.1.K6816 (ebook)
DDC [E]—dc23
LC record available at https://lccn.loc.gov/2024034349
LC ebook record available at https://lccn.loc.gov/2024034350

ISBN 9780593533727 (hardcover)
ISBN 9780593533734 (paperback)
1st Printing

Manufactured in the United States of America

LSCC

Design by Nicole Rheingans | Text set in Cosmiqua Pro

This book is a work of fiction. Any references to historical events, real people, or real places are used fictitiously. Other names, characters, places, and events are products of the author's imagination, and any resemblance to actual events or places or persons, living or dead, is entirely coincidental.

The authorized representative in the EU for product safety and compliance is Penguin Random House Ireland, Morrison Chambers, 32 Nassau Street, Dublin D02 YH68, Ireland, https://eu-contact.penguin.ie.

*To Jennifer and Susan. I thank my lucky socks for your magic every day.*
*—K.K.*

*To the magic Bramblegoop team at Putnam, Nicole, Eileen, Susan, and Kyra.*
*—M.A.*

## CHAPTER ONE

"Fellow fairies," said Oona Bramblegoop, standing as tall as her six inches could make her, "joining the fairy council has been a dream come true. So when the head of the council asked me to revise the Fairy Binder, well, that was a dream come *truer*. Today, I bring you twelve additional rules. The first is . . . The first is . . ." Her mind went blank. Crudmuffin.

She shuffled through her note cards and dropped them all over the floor. Double crudmuffin. Oona should have this whole speech memorized by now. As the newest member of the council, she needed to be extra fairytastic. She needed to prove she belonged.

Luckily, she was still at home, practicing in front of the mirror. Oona picked up a bowl of cotton candy casserole and took a couple of bites. Cotton candy casserole—or Triple C, as she liked to call it—always helped her focus. Then she sorted through each card until she found the rule she needed. She cleared her throat and started again. "The first rule is—"

Just then, a kaleidoscope of butterflies flew in through her window, each carrying a ribbon. At the other end of all

the ribbons was a package wrapped in rainbow tissue paper. A present!

The butterflies dropped the package in Oona's hands and hovered near the ceiling. Oona guessed that they wanted to know

what was inside almost as badly as she did. They were social butterflies after all, and they were excited to go tell the other fairies what gift Oona Bramblegoop, Underwear Fairy, had received. She tore off the paper. There was a box covered in sparkly jewels. Who could this be from? It was her quarter birthday next week. Maybe her little cousin Horace had sent her something?

She lifted the lid and gasped. Inside was a fairy council ID card, laminated and everything, with Oona's picture and her name written in sparkly script across the top.

"Woo-hoo! Hot snickerdoodledogs!" Oona shouted, spinning around with the card held

FUN BUTTERFLY FACT: *Social butterflies spread the news and gossip of more than just fairies. They also share info on elves, mermaids, unicorns, and even slugs and frogs. However, they avoid sharing leprechaun news because leprechauns are such pranksters. When one leprechaun reported that his sister "had tooted so much, her butt fell off," the butterflies pretty much stopped listening to them altogether.*

high over her head. This was it! It was official. The butterflies swirled around her and went out the window. She knew that every fairy in Blackberry Bog would know about her special card quicker than she could say *pixie kicks*, and that was fairy fine with her.

Before today, Oona had thought that the best day of her life was when she met Lucy, the one and only Tooth Fairy. Oona had always been in awe of Lucy. Plus, once Lucy learned about Oona's talent for providing protective underwear that kept the wearer from falling down with AUTO WEDGIE power, she had helped Oona be named the official Underwear Fairy. They had worked as a team from then on. They had become best friends!

But lately, Lucy had been too busy to be besties. Oona wasn't sure what she was busy *with*, but whatever it was, they weren't working on it as a team.

Oona's face got hot with the thought of another day feeling left out. She pressed the ID card against her cheek. It felt cool and smooth and wonderful.

Oona had an important meeting with the fairy council. She would be busy, too.

Turning back to the mirror, Oona tucked the card in her pocket and then pretended she was talking to an imaginary fairy. "You're all out of glitterberry muffins? What a shame. You don't have any left at all? Not even for a member of the"—card flash—"fairy council? Oh, you've found one for me? How lucky."

Ooh, she loved this ID card.

And she loved making up new rules. One of the best parts was it didn't even need magic.

Magic was tricky for Oona. Her magic always came out sort of sideways. At her first fairy council brunch, Oona had magicked up napkins. The spell seemed simple enough, but when all the members unfolded their napkins to eat, she was horrified. The napkins were shaped like underwear! Seeing Molly, the head of the fairy council, with a pair of underwear tucked under her chin made Oona want to crawl into a mole hole. She was relieved when Molly laughed it off, but she definitely didn't feel like she belonged *that* day.

But then Molly had decided that adding rules to the Fairy Binder was an important part of the preparations for Blackberry Bog's yearly Unicorn Reunion, and that Oona should do the job. Oona couldn't believe her luck. She had always been full of ideas, and now ideas were all she needed to please Molly.

Plus, Molly seemed to love each rule Oona made up more than the last. She was becoming Molly's right-hand fairy!

Uh-oh. Oona had been so caught up in her thoughts, she'd lost track of the time. The fairy council meeting had already started!

## CHAPTER TWO

Oona grabbed her note cards and her wand. Then she flitted out the door and skimmed down the spiral staircase leading from her fairy nest to the ground. Halfway down, she had to jump over a slug sunning itself on the steps. Two more slugs slid along the handrail. And near the bottom of her stairs, there was a whole

*Now, if only I had a lemonade with an umbrella in it.*

slew of slugs! That could only mean one thing—her little cousin Horace must be close by. He had replaced her as Slug Fairy after all.

"Horace? Horace!" she called, checking behind the tree trunk.

"Coming!" a clump of bushes called back in Horace's voice. She parted the leaves and there he was, hip-deep in brambles.

"What are you doing in there?" asked Oona.

"Taking a shortcut?" Horace shrugged.

"I see. Are you stuck?"

"Not me. It's this big old thing!" Horace was tugging a wagon behind him, and it had gotten wedged in between two extra-bushy branches.

"Well, I'm in a hurry, but I have time for one spell." Oona raised her wand to help him out.

"I really just need a hand—" Horace blurted, but Oona was already saying magic words.

"Hickory dickory duck,
You've gotten something stuck,
But if those branches sway,
They'll get out of the way!"

Suddenly, Oona was almost knocked over by a line of ducks pulling a cannon. They all climbed into the cannon but one, who struck a match and lit the cannon's fuse.

∽ When Fairies Go Too Far ∽

"Uh-oh," said Oona, plugging her ears. Sideways magic was often needlessly noisy. Yes, she had mentioned a duck, but why the cannon? Argh. Horace covered his eyes.

The fuse burned down, and *BOOM*, ducks rocketed by Horace on both sides, flattening down all the tangling sticks and leaves as they zoomed past.

"Am I dead?" Horace asked, his eyes still covered.

"Not a scratch," said Oona. A messy spell, for sure, but it worked.

"Thanks, Oo," he said. He dropped his hands, grinned, and started to pull the wagon again.

"What's in there, anyway?" she asked. "I hope it's not slugs—they'll be completely terrified!"

"Nope." He reached into the wagon, and after pulling out a stray duck, he showed her a giant book. "It's the new Fairy Binder. I just got my copy." Horace loved reading the Fairy Binder and memorizing all the rules. It was his hobby.

"Wow, I didn't realize it had gotten quite so big," Oona said.

"It's over a thousand pages," Horace said, rubbing his neck.

"Well, we have been adding things to get ready for the reunion. More fun for you, though, right, Horace? Lots of cool new rules to memorize."

Horace shook his head. It suddenly seemed like he didn't think the binder was as fun as he used to. "Actually, Oo, I wanted to ask you about some of these new ones."

Oona decided this was an ID-card-flashing opportunity. "Oona Bramblegoop, fairy council member, happy to help!" She presented Horace with the card. She even did a little salute. She thought Horace would giggle, but he didn't. He just handed the card back to her.

Then Horace heaved the big binder open toward the back and flipped a few pages. "Here. Rule Number 1,001: No magic allowed in the tying of shoes?"

Oona had thought up that one last week. Molly had loved it so much, she'd given Oona a sparkle sticker.

"It's just common sense, Horace. If a fairy is old enough to have their magic, they're definitely old enough to be able to tie their own shoes," Oona said.

"I guess so," Horace replied, biting his lip. "But even I sometimes forget what comes after making the laces into bunny ears. A little magic just helps at the end, you know?"

"We want the unicorns to be impressed when they visit," Oona told him, repeating

FUN FAIRY FACT: *Stickers work differently in the fairy world. Instead of sticking it onto something, fairies can hang a sticker in midair. They just take the backing off and place the sticker in any open space. It's great for decorating disco dances.*

what Molly had been saying for weeks. Then she added, "So every fairy must put their best foot forward . . . with shoes they tied themselves."

Horace thumbed through the pages again. "Rule Number 1,126? All fairies must wear stripes on Snorgleday? That's just weird."

Oona huffed. "Not weird. Fun. Do you not like fun all of a sudden?"

"Well, okay, but what about this one?" he said, pointing at the top of the page. It said: *Rule #1,225: The first two rows of the Grand Fairy Theater are reserved for fairy council members only.* "Why do we need that?"

"If you don't like that one, maybe I can improve it. I can try to get Molly to change

FUN FAIRY FACT: *Snorgleday is the eighth day of the fairy week. It comes after Sunday and before Monday, so fairies always have a three-day weekend! Fairies like to spend this day either snoring or snuggling, or, preferably, both.*

it to 'fairy council members *plus guests.*' Then you can sit with me!"

"That's not it, Oo. It's that . . . Well, it doesn't seem fair."

Oona didn't like all of these questions. She was just doing what the head of the council had asked her to do! To help all of fairydom! Why did silly old Horace always have to read every last word of the Fairy Binder, anyway?

"The reasons for some of these rules are on a need-to-know basis," she said finally. "And you definitely don't need to know."

"But—"

"I've got to get to work." She flapped her wings and rose off the ground.

"Think about it!" called Horace after her.

But Oona wasn't going to think about it. She had big responsibilities to get to that were too important for Horace to understand.

She headed toward the fairy council meeting place, which was high up on a cliff. Well, technically it was on a group of little clouds next to a high cliff. The last leg of the journey there was up a magical escalator made entirely out of wildflowers. But when she got there, it was so crowded with scolding frogs, she couldn't even see the bottom steps. This was going to make her late for sure.

What in fairydom was going on?

## CHAPTER THREE

"Excuse me, pardon me, coming through, official fairy council member here," Oona said, flashing her ID card as she squeezed in between ribbiting frogs. Oona used to be a little scared of the scolding frogs because they were often coming to scold *her*. But now her fairy council status made her bold. Scolding frogs were devoted to Molly, so they respected the council.

When she got to the top, she saw what all the frogs were doing here. There was a long line of fairies who had been summoned for official scoldings. The new rules must have caught a lot of the fairy world by surprise.

"That will be a two-week wand suspension for violating Rule Number 1,001," Molly said over and over, banging her gavel. It still made a hard, cracking sound even though she was banging it against a puff of cloud. Oona was surprised by the punishments. Two weeks seemed like an awfully long time for a little shoe-tying magic.

Her mind flashed back to her last wand suspension, and she shuddered. Having no magic was the worst, even if your magic was as unpredictable as Oona's. Maybe Horace was right about that rule. Or, she argued with herself, maybe the problem was just that these fairies had been lazy about learning to tie their shoes. At the end of the two weeks, they would get their wands back AND they would be great at shoe tying, all thanks to her.

One after another, fairies lost their wand privileges. Looking at their sad faces as they left made Oona's tummy twist.

But being on the fairy council meant she had to be strong and serious about the rules, right? She untangled her tummy and went to stand next to Molly.

After what seemed like a frillion fairies had been punished, Molly banged her gavel with a flourish. "The last item we have time for today is more new rules. Raise your hand to vote yes for Oona Bramblegoop's rule additions." Molly thrust her hand high in the air, and after a moment, all the other members followed her example.

"But don't you want to hear what they are first?" Oona said, taking out her note cards. "I've prepared a short speech—"

"You can just leave them with the frogs. I'm sure they're fine," Molly interrupted.

"But—"

"An additional rule is a good rule, that's what I say. And, Oona, your ideas are always just right." Then Molly banged her gavel to end the meeting.

Oona's body felt all scrambled up inside. She loved that Molly had given her such a glowing compliment, but she was disappointed that she had spent all that time on her speech for nothing. Plus, the fact that Molly had voted in rules without even knowing what they were itched at the corners of Oona's brain. And if she added to that all the things that Horace had said . . . something was off. She really wanted to talk to Lucy about all of this.

"Now that we've got all our business out of the way, we can spend some—what do humans call it?—*quality time* together," Molly said to Oona as the other fairy council members headed down the escalator. "I've got to give all the scolding frogs a bath. Why don't you wash and I'll dry?"

Oona bit her lip. She didn't think she could stay there another minute without all her disappointments and doubts turning into sloppy wet tears in front of Molly. Not to mention that the scolding frogs gave her the creeps. She had to get out of there.

"I'd love to, Molly, but I'm supposed to meet

up with the Tooth Fairy," Oona lied. "I can't be late."

Molly frowned. "Suit yourself," she said, then turned away to start gathering up frogs.

Oona rushed down the escalator, taking deep breaths to clear her head. Lucy could help her sort this whole rule situation out. As the Tooth Fairy, Lucy was the most important fairy of them all. She had won the VIF (Very Important Fairy) Award one hundred years in a row! And this last time, she had shared the trophy with Oona! The memory always made Oona blush.

FUN FAIRY FACT: *Being voted VIF comes with a lot of perks. In addition to the title and a big golden trophy, winners also get their portrait on a fairy stamp and a lifetime supply of gummy bears delivered to them by actual bears. Best of all, VIFs can always cut to the front of the line at the dentist. (Fairies really love the dentist. You can read that FUN FAIRY FACT in* Newbie Fairy.*)*

First Oona checked Lucy's nest, but she wasn't home. Then she went to the wishing well, and past the bog, and even looked around Rainbow Road, where the leprechauns lived. No Lucy. Why was she so hard to find these days?

*Where would I go if I were very important?* thought Oona. She knew that answer right away. She'd go to the Grand Fairy Theater and daydream about all the times she'd won the VIF Award there.

But apparently, Lucy didn't daydream the same as Oona, because the theater was empty.

Oona decided to go home and take a snuggle break under her covers until she got a new idea. Then, as she was passing the Chocolate Cave, at last she saw Lucy at the entrance.

"Oh, good, you're just the fairy I need! I've been looking for you!" Lucy said, giving Oona a hug.

"Really?" Oona squeaked. Things felt better already. "What's up?"

Lucy flicked her wand, and some paper and a pencil appeared. "I'm writing an official letter to Molly to tell her to cool it with these silly new rules. You spend a lot of time with her. What would you say to convince her to get rid of them all?"

Get rid of them all?! Oh no. First Horace, and now Lucy?

"The rules are *not* silly," Oona said. "They're for the Unicorn Reunion. And a more perfect fairy world."

Lucy shook her head. "I know we want everything to be fairytastic for the reunion, but how fairytastic can it be with so many fairies on wand suspension?"

*That's true,* thought Oona. But then her stubborn voice spoke up before she could stop it. "Which is exactly why fairies should be studying the new Fairy Binder."

"You sound like Molly," Lucy said.

"What's wrong with that?"

Lucy magicked the paper and pencil away again, and looked hard at Oona. "Everything! Molly has a tendency to get carried away with bossypants nonsense. You know that."

Oona looked at the ground. "I think you've got it wrong about Molly."

"I don't think so. I looked at the new Fairy Binder."

"And?"

"And don't you think the rules should be more about things like treating others with kindness and less about things we can't wear or do or say?"

Oona felt sparkly fairy tears welling up in her eyes. What was happening? She had come to Lucy for advice, and now they were arguing! Her insides felt like they'd been stuffed into her skin backward.

"If you're such a kindness fan, how about treating me with kindness instead of criticizing? I've been working really hard on that binder," Oona said, brushing the tears away.

"You wrote those rules?"

Oona nodded, snuffling.

"Oh, Oona, I'm sorry. I didn't realize," Lucy said. "I'm sure it was a lot of work, but . . . Listen, it's not personal. I'm just trying to think about what's best for Blackberry Bog."

"You're just jealous, is what it is." The words came flying out. "At least Molly appreciates me." Oona turned and started half flying, half stumbling away.

"Oona, wait!" Lucy called after her, but Oona kept going. She knew she was messing things up with Lucy, but she couldn't stand hearing all her favorite people say she was full of bad ideas.

Just then, her extra fairy perception started pinging loudly. Marco, the first human child

she had ever given protective underwear to, was signaling her in a major way.

A human emergency felt like a breath of fresh cinnamon-scented air. With a human emergency, what she should do wasn't so confusing. This would set her straight. If fairies weren't appreciating her work in her new job, at least she could still do her old job well. At the very least, Marco still needed her.

There was just one teensy wrinkle. Going to the human world during the daytime was strictly forbidden in one of the very first Fairy Binder rules. In fact, she'd been in trouble for that very thing before. But Oona didn't see what else she could do.

Marco needed her, she explained to herself. Even more than that, she needed to get away from all these judgy fairies.

No big deal. She just wouldn't get caught.

## CHAPTER FOUR

Oona went behind the magical waterfall and snuck down the twisty slide to the human world. But when she arrived at Marco's windowsill, all she saw was a pile of pillows and blankets. Shoot. She had been hoping to see Marco, but if he wasn't there, she would just have to leave the new pair of undies and go.

She raised her wand. Her feelings came pouring out along with her spell.

"Lucy and Horace seem
so full of doubt.

They don't understand that
I live to help out.

But Marco has always been
kind and not snooty,

So he gets new undies
and a safer patootie!"

*POOF!* A protective pair of undies appeared at the end of her wand. At the same time, a blue flannel sheet rose into the air like a huggable ghost. "Oona, is that you?" That wasn't a ghost. That was Marco! Oona peeked her head under the sheet.

"Hi!" he said. "I was building a fort, but it kept falling down."

"Good thing it's made out of soft things, then. Especially if you're needing new protective underwear."

"Oh, I don't need underwear."

"You don't? Then why was my EFP sounding the alarm?"

"I needed to show you something. Look." Marco walked over to his window and pointed. Oona hovered next to him and followed his finger. A glowing crescent moon was growing brighter in the gathering dusk.

"The moon?" she asked.

Marco moved his finger a little to the right. To her horror, Oona now saw something else in the sky. It was an unmistakable chunk of Blackberry Bog.

"Soggy shortbread! The fairy world is visible! This is a disaster!"

"That's why I called you," Marco said, his eyebrows coming together with worry. "I knew something was wrong."

"Thank you so much, Marco. You are a true friend of the fairies."

"Why do you think we can see it all of a sudden? What happened?" he asked.

Oona shook her head. Blackberry Bog was usually kept invisible by the magical combination of slug slime, fairy magic, and a little secret spice from the Grand fairies. She knew that the slugs were still doing their job because she had just helped Horace with his slime collecting. But what about the magic? Uh-oh. What if all these wand suspensions had created a magic shortage?

"I might have gone too far with something," Oona said, biting her lip.

"That happened to me with the popcorn popper once," Marco said, nodding. "I needed extra snacks for a movie marathon, so I put the whole jar of kernels in the popper. Whoa. My mom was right—more is not always better. Do you think you can fix it?"

"Maybe." Oona needed to talk to Molly ASAP. If they gave the suspended fairies their wands back, it could reset the magical balance. At least, she hoped it would.

"Thanks again, Marco. I've got to fly!" And she double-timed it to Blackberry Bog.

Oona had just gotten off the top of the twisty slide when she heard a stern voice.

FUN FAIRY FACT: *Grand fairy is the most advanced stage of a fairy's life. Not only can Grands make magic so easily that they don't need to bother with spells or wands at all, but sometimes they can get so stuffed with magic that they have to tuck away the extra in simple objects. It's always fun to peek inside cookie jars, jewelry boxes, and even in the ends of toilet paper rolls at a Grand's house, just to find whatever little bits of magic are hidden there.*

"When the frogs told me there was daytime slide usage, I certainly never expected to see a member of the fairy council."

Wincing, Oona turned toward the voice. It was Molly.

Crud on a cracker.

## CHAPTER FIVE

"THIS IS AN OFFICIAL SCOLDING," a frog boomed at Oona.

"Oh, shh. She knows what this is," said Molly.

"I can explain," Oona said. She was sure that once Molly heard about how part of Blackberry Bog was showing, she wouldn't care that Oona had gone down the slide in the daytime. Breaking that rule was a teensy-weensy problem; the exposure of the fairy world was a huge honker of a problem.

The scolding frogs that surrounded Molly made disapproving ribbits, but Oona continued. She explained the terrible news, waiting for Molly to jump into action. But Molly did not act at all the way Oona had expected.

"So humans can see Blackberry Bog. So what?" Molly said.

"So what?! So it will mess up the Sniccup!"

The Sniccup was the name of the delicate balance between the fairy and human worlds. With this balance, the wonder and mystery of fairies gave humans the ability to dream, and human dreams powered the fairies' ability to fly. Oona was sure that someone who was in charge of a lot of important fairy stuff, like Molly, would definitely do anything to protect the Sniccup.

**FUN FAIRY FACT:** *The Sniccup got its name because of a small side effect: Whenever a human sneezes more than three times in a row, a fairy gets the hiccups, and vice versa.*

Molly crossed her arms. "You didn't seem very worried about the Sniccup when you went down to visit a human child in the middle of the day."

Oona's face turned the color of a ripe strawberry. "Marco is an exception," she mumbled.

"How convenient," said Molly.

Oona's hopes for help were falling faster than a troll doing a cannonball. She tried again. "Once we're exposed to the humans, there will be nothing wondrous about leaving a tooth under your pillow at night and finding money in its place in the morning. The Tooth Fairy will just seem like a very short delivery person."

Molly actually laughed. "So what if humans won't be fascinated with Lucy anymore? So what if they don't write books about her or try to stay awake at night to catch a glimpse of her? So your BFF won't be famous. That does not matter to me. Not everyone is *obsessed* with the Tooth Fairy like you are."

Oona was stung. "I'm not obsessed."

"Please. You're so obsessed, you track her down even when I put scarcity magic on her—" Molly suddenly seemed to second-guess what she was saying. "I mean, you're just always following her around," she corrected herself.

But the confession hadn't slipped past Oona. "You put scarcity magic on Lucy?" No wonder she had been so hard to find lately! "Why would you do that?"

Molly shrugged. "That's on a need-to-know basis," she said.

If the fate of the fairy world hadn't been at stake, Oona would have pushed to get to the bottom of Molly's sneakiness, but right now Oona needed her help too badly. "You say that Blackberry Bog being visible doesn't matter to you, but what about the fact that when the humans see it, they'll all come up here to investigate with their big stomping

When Fairies Go Too Far

feet and swinging arms, and everything will get smooshed or smashed or both?"

"No, they won't."

"How can you be so sure?"

"Because we can stop them."

"But how?"

Molly smiled a little then. She carefully tucked her hair behind her ears and checked to see if her fingernails were clean. She seemed to be enjoying herself. "By getting rid of the only way up here. Or down," she said quietly. "By doing away with the magical twisty slide for good."

Oona felt like she'd just been socked in the stomach with a unicorn's horseshoe.

## CHAPTER SIX

**Oona's brain was** buzzing as she flew from one end of Blackberry Bog to the other. She had barely heard Molly and the frogs as they doled out their scolding and penalty for going down to the human world in the daytime: a two-week wand suspension of every type of magic except underwear protection.

But would she even need underwear protection magic soon? If the council demolished the twisty slide, she wouldn't be able to get to the children who needed protecting. Oona couldn't let that happen. She couldn't let the connection between humans and fairies be broken.

The first thing Oona needed to do was apologize to Lucy and Horace. They had been so right! Oona had been sticking her head in stubborn sand. She just hoped they would forgive her.

She planned to start with Lucy and then go find Horace, but when she got to Lucy's nest, Horace was already there. She could see the two of them eating glitterberry cake through the window. Since when had they started hanging out without her? She strained to hear what they were saying but couldn't. Every few sentences, though, she thought she heard her name. Were they talking about her?

Her wings curled. Half of her wanted to get mad, but then she reminded herself

she was there to apologize. She needed her friends now more than ever.

She took a deep breath and knocked on the door. When Lucy answered, Oona spoke right away, before either of them could say anything that might make her feel worse.

"I came to say I'm sorry. To you, too, Horace. I've been a foolish fairy. I was too busy with my fairy council meetings and fancy ID card to pay attention to what was really happening. But you both knew things were going wrong, and I'm so sorry I didn't listen sooner, because now everything's terrible and it's all my fault and I need your help to fix it." Then she filled them in about the hole in the protective magic underneath Blackberry Bog and Molly's plan to break the connection between fairies and humans altogether, which would make the problem much, much worse.

Finally, she took a breath and looked at her feet. Did her friends think she was a total ogre? Had they teamed up against her? Or would they give her another chance?

"Oh, Oo," said Horace, throwing his arms around her in a big hug. He was a little bit sticky from the cake, but on this particular day, Oona didn't mind. "You're not foolish. You're fairytastic! Now, tell me how to help, and I'm there!"

Just make sure he's home in time to sing slug songs before bed.

Oona hugged him back. "Thanks, Horace." Then they both looked at Lucy.

"Horace is right. You're not foolish. But you wouldn't have exactly won a listening contest the last time I talked to you," Lucy said, pouring herself some glitterberry juice.

"I know. All I can say is I'm sorry and I'll try not to let that happen again."

Oona and Horace held their breath as Lucy downed the whole glass of juice. Then, as she placed the cup back on the table, Oona saw a twinkle form in Lucy's eye. "So what's the plan?" Lucy said, clapping her hands. Phew.

"I've been noodling on that," said Oona, suddenly filled with energy. "Lucy, do you still have that little cloud? The one the Weather Fairy gave you for your birthday?"

"You mean Thor?" asked Lucy. "Of course."

"Aw, I didn't know he had a name," said Horace.

"You can't have a pet as cool as Thor and not name him eventually," Lucy replied.

"Good point," said Horace. "Does Thor still live in that little Tupperware?"

"That's his cozy spot for naps. But the rest of the time, he likes to float around my bathroom. I think he thinks the shower is his mom. It's cute. Impossible to find a dry towel, though."

"I do remember him being pretty drippy," Horace said, nodding.

"Anyway," said Oona, "I thought maybe Thor could help us cover up the exposed parts of fairydom. So that the fairy council

FUN FAIRY FACT: *Clouds are everywhere in the fairy world, and they're used as seats, pillows, and even transportation. But only the Weather Fairy can bring a cloud to life, which is how she gets them to help her block the sun or bring on storms. She can also bring lightning bolts to life, which is why she's in charge of all the fireworks shows.*

doesn't make any hasty decisions about our danger level."

"I thought exposed parts were the Underwear Fairy's business," said Horace, giggling at his own joke. "And by exposed parts, I mean butts."

"We get it, Horace," Oona said. "But seriously"—she turned back to Lucy—"would that work?"

Lucy thought for a minute. "Thor is too small to cover an area that large . . ." Then she brightened. "We'll just go to the Weather Fairy and see if she can make us a great big cloud."

Shoot. Oona blushed. "I don't think that's an option right now."

"Uh-oh. Let me guess—the Weather Fairy's wand was suspended?"

Oona ducked her head and nodded.

Lucy sighed, but she put her arm around Oona and squeezed. "All right. Let's go see what we can do."

The three fairies headed to Lucy's bathroom and found Thor doing zoomies around the tub.

"Hi, Thor! How's my little buddy?" Lucy cooed. "You want to go for a walk?" Thor spritzed with excitement.

◯〜 When Fairies Go Too Far 〜◯

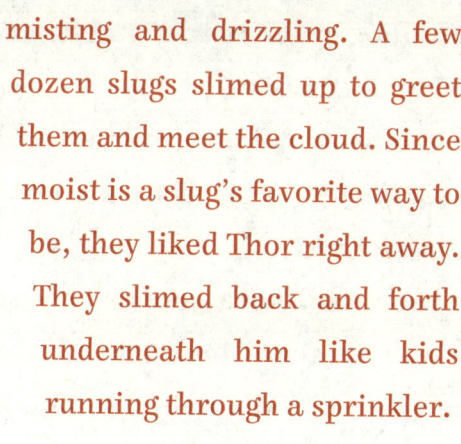

They headed off to the wettest part of the bog with Thor bouncing along above them, misting and drizzling. A few dozen slugs slimed up to greet them and meet the cloud. Since moist is a slug's favorite way to be, they liked Thor right away. They slimed back and forth underneath him like kids running through a sprinkler.

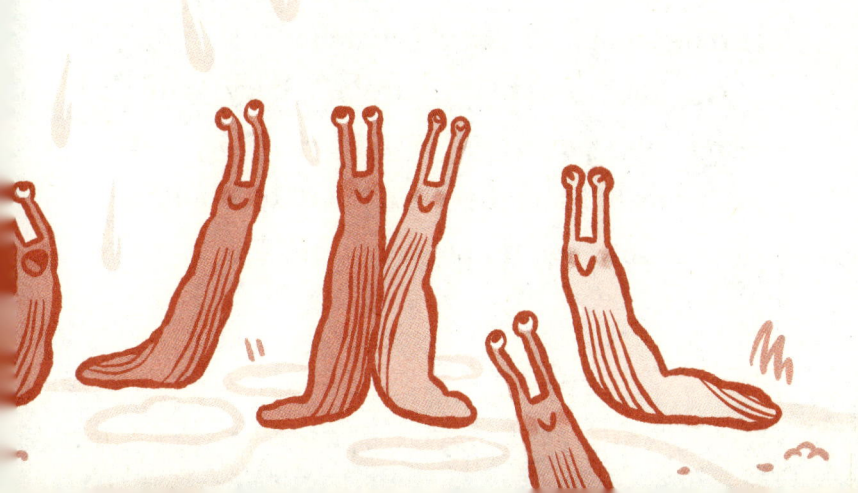

The fairies had just turned toward the Sky Hatch when Oona spotted a few nosy scolding frogs, partly hidden in the reeds, watching her.

"Molly can't know what we're doing," Oona said, nodding toward the frogs. "We need a distraction."

"Sounds like a job for my super slugs!" said Horace. He puckered up and sent out a silent slug whistle, and all the slugs smooshed themselves together into a slimy wall. Then the slug wall surrounded the frogs and peppered them with questions.

Once the frogs were busy, the three fairies surrounded a giant tree stump that had a top like the lid of a submarine. They all grabbed on to the circular handle.

"On the count of purple," Lucy said. "Pajamas, pancakes, PURPLE!" They all pulled as hard as they could, and the handle turned until the lid popped open. Then, one

## When Fairies Go Too Far

by one, they climbed onto the stump and lowered themselves down the ladder inside. Thor zipped along behind them. It was clear he liked to stay as close to Lucy as he could.

They came out underneath Blackberry Bog. Horace kept one hand on the ladder to help him hover in the sky, since his wings were still pretty new. The three fairies looked up. The bare patch looked even worse up close. Lucy and Horace were both speechless.

Finally, Oona said, "Well? What do you think?"

Lucy shook her head. "Oh, crudmuffin. It's huge!"

Horace squinted. "And I think it's growing."

## CHAPTER SEVEN

He was right. The view of the fairy world was inching wider and wider.

"What are we going to do?" Horace asked, his face scrunched up.

"This would be a great time for fairy dust if I still carried it," Lucy said. "It would help slow the growth of the hole."

"Why *don't* you carry it anymore?" Horace asked.

Lucy shrugged. "I always ended up going too far with it. But not to worry. I might be

able to magick up a way for Thor to expand so he can cover this whole area. I just need to make sure all that stretching won't hurt him."

When Thor heard that, he dumped about a gallon of water right on Horace's head and then tried to stuff himself inside Lucy's pocket. Horace shook himself dry like a dog.

Lucy patted Thor. "Now, don't soak yourself. I won't let anything happen to you."

Seeing Lucy comfort her little cloud gave Oona an idea.

"If Thor needs protecting, I can handle that," Oona said. She raised her wand.

"This little cloud made a rainstorm,
And this little cloud made some shade.
This little cloud made it misty,
And this little cloud wouldn't fade.

*"This little cloud grew much wider
While floating up high in the air,
And all of the stretching was easy
Because of his new underwear!"*

Immediately, a Thor-sized pair of underwear appeared on the end of Oona's wand.

"Ha! Well, this should be interesting," Lucy said. "Last I checked, Thor doesn't have any legs."

"That's okay," said Oona. "He just needs to improvise a little bit. Come here, little guy."

Oona held out the undies, and Thor pushed a puff of whiteness through each leg hole. He looked like a half-dressed sheep. After some wiggling, Thor's fluffiness hid the undies from view. He sprinkled a thank-you on Oona's head.

"Talk about wetting your pants." Horace giggled.

"Okay, Thor, time to be a big boy!" said Lucy, and with a flick of her wand, he began to grow, wider and wider, until he covered up the entire underside of Blackberry Bog.

"It's perfect!" Oona crowed. "Thor looks just like a regular old cloudy day in the human world."

Lucy held up her hand. "It's perfect, but it's temporary. We can't leave Thor stretched out down here forever. We've got to stop this problem at the source." She gave Thor one more pat. "You're doing great, little guy. I'll be back for you soon. Hang in there."

The three fairies skimmed back up the ladder and secured the lid of the stump.

"Oo, we've got to get rid of the extra rules in the Fairy Binder," said Horace. "That's the only way to bring back all the magic in the fairy world."

"Molly will never agree to that," Oona said. "I think she actually wants Blackberry Bog to be discovered by the humans. Then the council will have to agree to her plan to remove the twisty slide. Since Molly's never been to the human world, I think she's jealous of fairies like us who have. I don't know. But she definitely wants this magic shortage to continue."

"But Molly is the head of the fairy council. Is there a way to change the binder without her permission?" Lucy asked.

Oona sighed. "There used to be. But the fairy council just voted to change that. The new version of the binder needs Molly for everything."

"Crudmuffin," Horace said. "How do we get Molly's permission without getting Molly's permission?"

Suddenly, Oona clapped her hands. "Horace, you're a genius!"

Horace grinned. "That's me! Wait—why am I a genius?"

Oona laughed. "We need to get Molly's permission without Molly, right? Well, what if we went to Grand Bramblegoop instead?"

Horace crowed his approval, but Lucy needed catching up. "Wait, how can your Grand help?"

"She's a shape-shifter," Oona said, her wings flapping with pride. "She can turn into anything—a troll, a tricycle, even a triple-chocolate cheesecake!"

"Wow, that's advanced fairy magic," said Lucy.

"It can get a little confusing sometimes," said Horace. "But the good news is that her curly purple hair never changes. So if you're at a Bramblegoop family get-together and the corn on the cob has curly purple hair, you know not to eat it."

"Great. So your Grand can change into Molly, and then we can change the binder!"

Lucy rose into the air. "What are we waiting for? Let's head to the Big Banyan Tree before Thor gets as stretched out as an old bathing suit."

**FUN FAIRY FACT:** *All the Grand fairies live together in the oldest tree in Blackberry Bog—the Big Banyan Tree. Its roots spread through all of the fairy world, just a few inches underground. And it is through the roots that the Grands hear the hopes, wishes, and hurts of all the other fairies. That's why they have the strongest EFP. It's also why they send the best care packages.*

# CHAPTER EIGHT

After stopping on the other side of the bog to get Horace's wagon with the copy of the Fairy Binder, they flitted toward the tree. Soon Horace was lagging behind. Oona looked over her shoulder and stopped.

"Do you want me to take a turn pulling?" she asked.

"No, I've got it," Horace said. "I'm just a little worried."

"What about?"

"Impersonating another fairy is super-duper-extra against the rules, you know. I don't want to get Grandgoop in trouble."

Neither did Oona. But this was the only way. "Grandgoop is wise; she'll know how to stay out of trouble," said Oona.

But then it occurred to her that maybe Horace was worried about getting himself in trouble, too. She touched his arm. "Sometimes it's okay to break the rules if you're doing the right thing," she said. "We're saving children's ability to dream here. Not to mention our own wings."

Horace took a deep breath and nodded. "Let's keep going."

Soon, the Big Banyan Tree rose up in front of them, its trunk wide and smooth and its branches covered with twinkling lights, like the tree was wearing a dozen diamond necklaces.

"Oh no," Oona said suddenly.

"What is it?" asked Horace.

"A present! We forgot a present!" said Oona.

"Ooh, maybe I can magick one up!" Horace took out his wand. "Please, magic wand, can you help me make a present for my Grand?" Then he took a feather out of his pocket and tickled his nose while twisting up his face and holding his breath.

"What in fairydom is he doing?" asked Lucy, staring at Horace.

FUN FAIRY FACT: *It is a long-standing tradition that fairies bring a present when they visit a Grand. Grands are a little bit like crows and love to collect anything shiny or sparkly. So fairies often bring crystals or polished silver, but even a roll of tinfoil is an acceptable present.*

Oona shook her head and chuckled. "You don't want to know."

Horace grunted. Lucy looked at Oona, bewildered.

"Fine," Oona said. "He's trying to snoot. To snart. To sneeze and toot at the same time. That's how he makes magic."

Lucy's mouth dropped open.

AH-AH-AH-CHOO!

Horace sneezed while a little squeak escaped his other end. "Excuse me."

Lucy laughed. "I've heard of a puff of magic before, but this is a whole different level." She had to sit down, she was laughing so hard. On the ground next to her, Horace's magical creation sparkled. Lucy picked it up and turned it over in her hands.

"It's beautiful!" Lucy said. "What is it?"

"It's fossilized slug slime," Horace said. "Sort of like amber, but from slugs."

"Good job, Horace," said Oona. "Grandgoop will love it."

When they got to Grand Bramblegoop's door, it was already open, but the room appeared to be empty. Where was she? Then Oona heard a scrabbling sound from a low cupboard. When she opened it, a cute little hedgehog with a shocking head of purple curls hopped out.

"Why, hello, my little fairylets!" said the hedgehog. "How about a hug?"

Oona and Horace looked at each other. "Sure, Grandgoop," said Oona. "But do you think you could be a little less pokey first?"

"Oh, oopsies. I can't find my saltshaker, so I thought if I was the size of a saltshaker, I might have an easier time finding it," she said. "Can't make magic biscuits without a

pinch of salt." Then the little hedgehog nodded, and a river of sparkles shot from her curls, swirling straight toward the fairies. But before it reached them, it stopped in midair and boomeranged backward. The next thing they knew, their Grand was standing in front of them, her normal self. She looked like a sweet, older combination of Oona and Horace.

Suddenly, Grandgoop's eyes grew wide. She leaned in and whispered, "Just be cool and don't go bananas, but the VIF champion is standing right behind you!"

Oona smiled. "Oh, Grandgoop, I know that already. Lucy's our friend, remember?"

Grandgoop smoothed back her curls and blushed. "Well, then, any friend of my fairylets is a friend of mine. Come in, come in!"

After hugs and introductions, Horace pulled out the fossilized slug slime. "We brought you a present."

"Ooh, and so shiny! How did you know?" Grandgoop said.

Oona and Horace grinned at each other.

"Put it in my favorite shiny spot, where it can catch the sunlight, would you?"

Horace handed it to Oona, who placed the gift high on a shelf covered with sparkly objects, including a crystal saltshaker, which she gave to Grandgoop.

"Well, snickerdoodle, there it is!" She turned to Lucy. "They are just the goopiest little Bramblegoops, aren't they?"

"As goopy as they come," said Lucy, suppressing a giggle.

"Come, come sit down. Fill me in on the big problem that's been tickling my EFP all day."

The three fairies told Grandgoop everything. Then Horace heaved the new binder onto the table. Grandgoop flipped through it, gasping and tsking and sometimes chortling as she went.

When Fairies Go Too Far

When she got to the stripes rule, she threw back her head and laughed, while at the same time changing into a zebra with a curly purple mane. Her laugh transformed into a spirited neigh.

Lucy and Horace laughed, too, but Oona was quiet. She felt ridiculous. Why had she ever thought all these rules were a good idea? Oona had gobbled up whatever foolishness Molly had fed her, hook, line, and slug. Just so she could feel like she belonged. What a mistake. When her Grand saw Oona's eyes filling with tears, she turned back into herself.

"Don't worry, my little glitterbug," Grandgoop said. "We all get carried away sometimes. Why, I put a whole bottle of bubble bath in the tub once. Turns out more is not always better. So, how can I help?"

"Well, we have an idea," Oona said. "But I should tell you that it's very risky. If we're caught, you could get your magic suspended."

"Oh, my sugar snap, you think I'd worry about a little magic suspension? You should have seen me when I was a Newbie. I had a scolding frog at my feet every second Snorgleday!"

In that moment, Oona loved her Grand more than all the glitterberry cakes in Blackberry Bog.

Grandgoop stood up, fluffed out her curls, and smiled. "Now, let's go kick some Fairy Binder butt."

## CHAPTER NINE

Together, the four fairies set out for the fairy council cliff, Oona and Lucy beating their wings and skimming above the ground, Horace half running, half flitting with his frantic little flappers, and Grandgoop coasting on the breeze above them. When they got close to the flower escalator, they stopped.

"Okay, Grandgoop, it's time," said Oona.

"Show me what she looks like again?"

Oona took out her fairy council ID card. Her picture was on the front, but as head of the council, Molly had put her picture on the back. Oona had known this card was going to come in handy, but not like this.

Lucy snorted at the photo. "Classic. She even looks fussbudgety in her picture."

Grandgoop put on her fairy glasses and squinted at the card. "Got it," she said. The river of sparkles boomeranged, and suddenly, Molly was standing next to them. The resemblance was unsettling. The only thing that kept Oona from jumping right out of her skin was that *this* Molly had curly purple hair.

"You think the rest of the council will believe that Molly changed her hair?" asked Horace.

"To purple? Not exactly Molly's style," said Lucy.

"I can fix that!" Oona raised her wand. At the last second, she remembered her punishment: underwear magic only. This situation didn't call for her typical protection skills, but maybe if she worked underwear into the spell somewhere, it would be fine.

*"Look in a mirror, and what do you see?*
*Do I look like you, or do you look like me?*
*Grandgoop is Molly, except for her hair.*
*Let's fix up this problem without underwear!"*

"Hey! What the what?!" yelled Horace.

Oona looked over to see her cousin jumping around, yelping and clutching his shorts.

What was wrong with him? But she didn't have time to figure it out before a large washing machine appeared next to her, thumping loudly as it sloshed and spun. What was her sideways magic up to this time? She peered through the glass in the door.

"That washing machine stole my underwear!" Horace pointed. As if on cue, boxers with pictures of little slugs on them passed in front of the window.

"Oops. I was trying to tell my magic to *not* use underwear to solve the problem, but I think it heard *take away underwear* to solve the problem."

The washing machine spun faster and faster, and sparks began to fly out of it. Just as Oona was starting to fear it would explode, it slowed to a halt. Horace threw open the door to retrieve his underwear, but it was gone. In its place was a wig that looked exactly like Molly's hair.

Pulling the wig on and tucking in some stray curls, Grandgoop said, "Wonderful!"

And it was. It was perfect.

"Sorry, Horace," Oona said, biting her lip.

Horace shrugged. "If I have to go commando to save the fairy world, then that's what I have to do." He grinned.

"Just be careful," said Oona. Horace was very clumsy without his protective undies.

"Don't you worry about me. I'm not a baby Boggin anymore." He flexed his little muscles and then immediately tripped over his own feet. "I mean, I will."

The four fairies boarded the magical flower escalator to the top, where a scolding frog was sitting on a cloud puff, unrolling and rerolling his tiny scroll over and over. When he saw Grandgoop/Molly, he jumped to attention.

"Ah, good. You're here. Gather up the rest of the council for an emergency meeting immediately," Grandgoop/Molly said.

The little frog cocked his head to one side and then the other, the way a dog does when it hears a sound it doesn't recognize. Her voice! Grandgoop's voice did not sound like Molly's at all.

When Grandgoop saw how the frog was looking at her, she cleared her throat and took a step backward, directly into Horace, who was close at her heels. And without AUTO WEDGIE magic to keep him on his feet, they both tumbled to the ground. Several of Grandgoop's purple curls popped out from under the wig.

Oona jumped in front of them and started waving her official ID card back and forth in the frog's face, like she was trying to hypnotize him with it.

"Quick!" Oona said. "Molly has a rare case of fairy laryngitis, and we need to add all the new rules before she loses her voice altogether. So hop to it, or else we'll punish you for extra scroll-rolling."

This got the frog's attention, but he still didn't move.

Lucy stepped close to him. "Do you know who I am? What will the other scolding frogs say when they find out you kept the Tooth Fairy waiting for no reason?"

That did it. The frog saluted and hopped away as fast as his little legs could spring.

"Nice!" Oona said to Lucy.

Lucy smirked. "You too. You've gotten really good at being bossy since you joined the fairy council."

Oona's wings curled at the ends in embarrassment. "That was emergency bossiness, I promise. From now on, I'm going to listen more and tell fairies what to do less. Have I mentioned that I am really sorry about all this?"

Lucy gave her a quick hug. "I know, my friend. I was teasing, but I'll stop. I promise, too."

Just then, Grandgoop held her fingertips to her temples. "Ouch," she said.

"What's wrong?" asked Horace.

"EFP alert. It's a strange one, though. It feels like *the weather* is sending out an SOS, but that can't be right."

Oona and Lucy looked at each other. "Thor!" they said at the same time.

"I'll take care of it," Lucy said.

"I'll help!" said Horace. "I like that stormy little guy."

"And I'll stay and translate for Molly over here, since she clearly has fairy laryngitis," said Oona. The fairies tapped wands and parted ways.

By the time the other members of the fairy council started rolling up to the top of the magic escalator, Lucy and Horace were long gone. Grandgoop was seated on a large puff of cloud in the center of things, her purple strands tucked away under her wig. Oona sat to her right. Everything looked just like usual. At least, that's what Oona hoped.

## CHAPTER TEN

"Come in, come in," said Oona. "So sorry for the unscheduled meeting, but we have a problem."

Immediately, a flurry of concern rose up from the other fairy council members, who were settling into their cloud seats.

"Oh no!"

"What kind of problem?"

"What should we do, Molly?"

"Who is to blame for this problem?"

Oona hadn't realized the fairy council was such a high-strung bunch. "Please, calm down, it's nothing we can't solve," she said over the kerfuffle.

"Who are you to say?"

"We want to hear it from Molly!"

Oona tried to keep her voice confident and soothing. "Molly was in a singing contest and has fairy laryngitis, so I will be speaking for her today."

Grandgoop nodded at this, smiling at each fairy council member. The fairies all nodded back, seeming to believe this. Molly was very competitive.

---

**FUN FAIRY FACT:** *Fairy laryngitis is a rare condition. It is usually caused by losing a singing contest with a magical macaw. The macaw will keep three-quarters of your voice as a prize until it loses a contest to another creature. Then all the extra voices are released back to their rightful owners.*

"It has come to our—Molly's—attention that we are experiencing a magic shortage in Blackberry Bog," Oona continued. There were several gasps, so Oona paused until there was quiet again. "We need to reverse the wand suspensions to bring the magical balance back and keep the fairy world hidden and the Sniccup safe."

"Reverse!"

"How could we do that?"

"It's never been done!"

No wonder Molly always carried that gavel.

"Eh-hem. Quiet down, please. It's actually pretty easy." Oona recited the Fairy Binder rule that Horace had taught her: "Rule Number Eighty-Five: Any new rule may be deleted when everyone votes so no one feels cheated." Oona liked Rule #85. It rhymed, just like her magic spells.

With that, Grandgoop/Molly nodded at the Fairy Binder. Oona opened it up and read aloud. "Rule Number 1,241: No fairy may ride a Pegasus without first French braiding its mane. All in favor to delete?" Grandgoop/Molly and Oona held their hands high. The rest of the fairy council looked nervous, like they had suddenly found themselves getting onto a roller coaster that was a bit too loop-de-loopy. They looked from Oona to Grandgoop/Molly and back to Oona again.

"Come on, fairy friends!" Oona said, clapping her hands to snap them out of it. "More magic in Blackberry Bog is good for all of us!"

To her relief, they raised their wands, one by one. "Approved!"

Oona kept going, reading aloud every rule that didn't seem important, which was most of them. Soon they got into a rhythm, Oona reading and all the fairies voting, more quickly and enthusiastically each time. As each page of rules was erased, it ripped itself out of the binder, folded itself into a paper airplane, and flew away.

And as it flew, suspended magic wands would—*poof!*—appear and join the airplane in its path, like geese forming a V to head south for the winter. Except these wands were headed back to their fairies.

All the while, the binder grew slimmer and slimmer. Oona could almost feel the magic returning, crackling like electricity in the air around her. This was going to work! She was going to save the fairy world!

Suddenly, she heard a voice that made her toes curl up inside her shoes.

"What in all of fairydom is going on here?"

It was Molly. And boy, did she look mad.

# CHAPTER ELEVEN

The Fairy Binder snapped shut. All the fairies turned to see Molly at the top of the escalator, surrounded by scolding frogs, a crumpled paper airplane in her hand.

Molly's ears were red, and her striped hat was askew. Oona thought she might pop like a bubble, she looked so furious. In that moment, Oona realized that they should have also made a plan for what to do when Molly found out what they were up to.

But they hadn't thought that far ahead. And now it was too late.

For a long moment, nobody spoke. Finally, one of the fairy council members pointed and squeaked, "If that's Molly, then who is *that*?"

Molly stomped onto a puff of cloud and steered it up close to Grandgoop/Molly's face. She took out her magnifying glass and stared. Then she reached up and snatched the wig off of Grandgoop's head. Purple curls spilled out every which way. The rest of the fairy council gasped.

"An impostor!" Molly announced, holding the wig up high like a trophy. "She must be punished!"

When Fairies Go Too Far

Grandgoop yelped and turned into a bumblebee (with curly purple hair). Then she flew and hid deep inside one of the flowers on the escalator. Molly turned toward Oona.

"Hi, Molly, g-g-good to see you," Oona stammered. "I can explain. It's not what you think. I mean, it's a little bit what you think. The impostor thing was a mistake. That's my fault. It's just that the fate of the entire fairy world was at risk, and you were being so stubborn—"

"That's enough, Underwear Fairy. I will deal with you after I fix what you have broken." Molly waved her wand so fast, it looked like she was angry at the air. Within seconds, all the paper airplanes were flying back and piling up around the binder.

"Now, hold on, Molly," Oona said, her voice a little stronger. "Everyone except you just agreed that those rules are causing more fairy problems than they're solving. If you would only listen—"

"Everyone except me?! What does that mean, you and your precious Tooth Fairy friend? EVERYONE EXCEPT ME DOES NOT MATTER." Molly stopped pointing her wand at the sky and pointed it at Oona instead. Suddenly, Oona tasted marshmallow. She tried to speak but couldn't.

Molly had sealed her lips closed with super-sticky marshmallow creme.

Oona turned toward the escalator, wildly hoping that Lucy and Horace had returned. Oh, crudmuffin! The escalator was dumping a steady stream of scolding frogs onto the cliff, enough for a scolding frog army. And oh no! One of the frogs flicked his tongue into a flower and pulled out her Grand!

With a wild buzzing sound, Grandgoop managed to sting the sticky tongue. Then she flew straight up in the sky as the frog clamped his mouth shut. But she still wasn't safe because, at the same time, Molly sent a batch of cloud puffs over to the frogs. The frogs jumped on and began zooming toward the little bee.

Oona had to do something, but she still wasn't skilled enough to do magic without words; like all Newbies, she had to say her spells out loud.

*Although*, thought Oona, *how do I really know I can't do it if I haven't tried?*

There was one type of magic that Oona could do as naturally as falling off a bog log, and that type just might work. She closed her eyes. In her mind's eye, she saw a protective pair of undies, and she concentrated as hard as she could on that mental picture.

Nothing happened. Cruddy, cruddy crudmuffin.

Meanwhile, the other fairy council members were trying to reason with Molly. And one by one, she sealed their lips closed.

"The disrespect!" Molly howled, waving her wand all around. Scolding frogs jumped out of her way so she wouldn't accidentally seal their mouths shut, too. "You leave me no choice, disloyal fairies. It's time to add one final rule to the Fairy Binder. Rule Number 1,242: The head of the fairy council, aka me, Molly Malarkey, will now be in charge of

EVERYTHING!"

Suddenly, the warm chocolate chip cookie smell that always filled fairydom was swept away in a cold breeze. It was replaced by the smell of sour milk. Even the frogs froze for a moment.

What was Molly doing to the fairy world? Oona didn't think things could get much worse. Then the frogs started racing around on their clouds again, and Oona saw one of them swing a long-handled net and scoop up her Grand.

Oona tried to fly to her, but there were just too many frogs. Saving Grandgoop with magic was the only way.

What if she said the words of a spell through the marshmallow? Her wand knew her pretty well by now; maybe it could figure it out.

She closed her eyes and mumbled:

*"Darling, dumpling, sweetie pie,*
*Frogs can catch you in the sky.*
*But when you're scared and feeling small,*
*Undies hear the rescue call."*

It sounded more like humming, but in her mind the words were as clear as a freshly washed window. Oona opened her eyes.

It worked! There was the purple-haired bumblebee, wearing a tiny pair of bright-white undies. The underwear went into AUTO WEDGIE mode, and each wedgie lifted her up, up, up, out of the net and away from the frogs. Once she was in the clear, Grandgoop landed on the cliff's edge and quickly turned back into her uneatable self. Oona's worried shoulders relaxed.

Now that Grandgoop was safe, Oona was going to give those frogs a lecture about the importance of identifying shape-shifting fairies. But when she turned to them, she realized they couldn't understand her mumbling. The frogs wouldn't have listened to her anyway. They were too busy pointing at something and gasping.

Oona's gaze followed their froggy fingers straight to Molly.

She was still standing by the Fairy Binder, clutching her wand and looking furious, except for one important difference. She also had a pair of underwear around her ankles.

Uh-oh. Did Oona do that?

When Molly noticed everyone's eyes on her, she looked down. Blushing, she grabbed the undies and pulled them up. Instantly, her face changed. She looked calm and peaceful, even though she had to pluck out several wedgies in a row from the new underwear.

"For fairy's sake, Oona!" Molly said, looking at the marshmallow mess on Oona's face. "That was not fairy-like of me at all. Here . . ." Molly waved her wand and unsealed all the fairies' mouths. "Now, that's better."

"Thanks, Molly," Oona said, confused by this sudden change. "Does this mean we can talk about the rules in the Fairy Binder?"

"Oh yes . . . the Fairy Binder." Molly's eyes filled with tears. "I haven't been very reasonable, have I?" She waved her wand, and a box of tissues appeared. She blew her nose long and hard. Then she started crying so much, she had to sit down.

Grandgoop came over to Oona, and Oona whispered to her, "Is this some sort of trick?"

Her Grand cocked her head to the side. "Those were your magical undies Molly put on, weren't they? The ones that provide protection magic?"

"Yes," Oona said. "But I don't think she's crying over a wedgie."

"Let me ask you, then," said Grandgoop. "Why did you help Molly make all those rules in the first place?"

"I don't know. Because I wanted to do something important."

"But why?"

Oona looked around as if the answer were hanging in the air. "I guess because I wanted Molly and the rest of the council to think I was good enough to be a council member. I wanted them to like me."

"Ah," said Grandgoop, nodding. "I think Molly might want the same thing."

"But what does that have to do with underwear?"

"The part of Molly that needed protection

wasn't her body. It was her heart. And now that her heart feels safe, her hard outer coating is melting away like an M&M. Instead of bossy Molly, we can see soft and squishy Molly."

## CHAPTER TWELVE

Whoa, Oona thought, her Grand was so wise! Oona hoped that her own EFP would grow that sensitive one day.

"Should I talk to her?" Oona asked Grandgoop. But she already knew the answer.

Oona got close to Molly and touched her hand. "Are you okay?"

"Yes. No. I don't know! I don't usually cry. It must be allergies! Have you been eating cucumbers? I'm allergic to cucumbers."

## When Fairies Go Too Far

"Gosh, Molly, I'm not an expert, but I think it might be feelings, not cucumbers. How do you feel?"

"I feel . . . I feel . . . LONELY!" Molly sobbed loudly. She blew her nose again. Then she handed the tissue to Oona.

Oona tucked it in her pocket. "But you're the head of the fairy council! Nothing

FUN FAIRY FACT: *Everything that comes from fairies is sweet and sparkly—even their snot! Fairy snot is filled with glitter and is often used to decorate fairy greeting cards. Don't worry, though. Germs don't exist in the fairy world.*

important can happen in fairydom without you. How could you be lonely?"

Molly shook her head. "Being in charge doesn't mean you're not lonely. Everyone else seems to have good friends—I see how tight you and the Tooth Fairy are—but I don't. After you joined the council, I really thought you and I would be friends, but you always left after meetings. Even when I made Lucy more scarce—sorry about that, by the way—you still wanted to find her instead of hanging out with me. The only company I end up with are these guys." She waved at the frogs, who were still in shock. "And they're not happy unless they're busy scolding somefairy."

The pieces were starting to click together in Oona's brain. That's why Molly kept adding rules: so she and the frogs would have something to do and someone to do it with. But ending all fairy-human connection? What had Molly hoped to get from that?

## When Fairies Go Too Far

"Feeling lonely is yucky with a capital *Y*," Oona said, rubbing Molly's back the way Horace did when Oona was snuffling. "But why did that make you want to stop contact with the human world?"

"That's where your and Lucy's friendship really started, isn't it? A lot of fairy friendships form down in that magical place, and I'm . . . never . . . THERE." The last word came out as a long sob. Soft and squishy Molly sure was different from regular Molly.

Oona wrapped her arm around Molly. "Now, listen. I think it would be fairytastic to hang out with you anytime."

"You already have a friend." Molly sniffed.

"A fairy can have more than one friend!"

"Not really."

"Sure they can! We're going to get you lots of friends! I'm sure we can find more fun things for you to do in between council meetings and fun fairies to do them with. But you have to stop with all the punishments."

"You'll hang out with me anytime?" Molly looked up at Oona with hope. Then she frowned and whispered, "But what will your friends and family say?"

She pointed toward the escalator. Horace and Lucy had finally arrived at the top,

their faces filled with questions. Thor was with them, and he'd clearly had a big day—Lucy was wearing him around her shoulders while he napped. Horace gave Oona a thumbs-up, and Oona knew magic must be returning to the fairy world.

"They'll be your friends, too!" Oona said, waving them over. She nodded hard at Horace and Lucy as she said, "You'll hang out with Molly, right? She can be friends with all of us, can't she?"

Horace grinned. "Of course!"

Lucy didn't say anything. She looked doubtful. Oona realized she should have expected that. Lucy and Molly had been competitive for a long time.

Finally, Lucy said, "I don't know. It's hard to trust fairies who are always getting carried away. They're very . . . unpredictable."

Lucy's words struck Oona in a sensitive spot in her chest. It was suddenly more important than ever that Lucy forgive Molly.

"Lucy, if there's one thing I know about you, it's that you are great at giving fairies second chances. You gave me a second chance when I took things too far, and I am so thankful. I know you can do that for Molly, too. She'll work hard every day to deserve it. Right, Molly?"

Molly took off her hat and placed it over her heart. Then she said in the quietest voice Oona had ever heard from her, "I would be honored to be your friend, Lucy."

Lucy sighed and rubbed her forehead. Then

she laughed. "All right, all right," she said. "What are fairies for? Fairy group hug!"

"Ooh, and we can talk all about binder business," Horace said when they finished hugging. "Binder history, and different font choices for rules, and which rules have led to other rules—"

"Well, that conversation might be pretty short, Horace," said Molly. "Because Oona and I"—she smiled at Oona—"we have decided to revise the Fairy Binder back to basics."

Oona clapped her hands. "Fairytastic! You mean it?"

Molly nodded. "You're right, Oona. The fairy council should be about encouraging more magic, not less."

"And what about . . ." Oona was almost afraid to say the words. "What about the twisty slide?"

Molly laughed, making Oona jump in surprise. "Oh, I could never destroy the connection with the human world. What would happen to the Sniccup? I like flying too much. Besides, the Dust Bunny Fairy would put all her dust bunnies right on my toothbrush if I stopped her from her doing her job."

That was a relief.

Molly clapped her hands. "Let's go make sure all the fairies get their wands back!"

The other fairies on the council cheered, and Oona cheered loudest of all. But as their cheering calmed down, they heard boos behind them.

No scolding? The scolding frogs did not seem to like this idea at all.

Molly wrinkled her nose. "They're so high-maintenance."

Grandgoop had been watching this whole conversation. Now she stepped forward and said, "I might have an idea these little green guys will love."

# CHAPTER THIRTEEN

When Oona got to the Big Banyan Tree the following Frimpday, it was crawling with frogs. They were certainly busy. More importantly, they seemed very happy. And the happiest of all was a frog sitting next to a big basket. A frog with a thick mop of curly purple hair.

"Grandgoop!" called Oona, and she flapped up to her shape-shifting Grand.

"Hello, my little sugar snap!" Grandgoop gave her a slightly sticky hug.

"I have to say, whatever your idea was, it worked. The scolding frogs look like they're having a great time!"

"Ah-ah-ah," said her Grand, shaking her head and wagging a froggy finger. "They are no longer scolding frogs. Who needs all that scolding? Allow me to introduce . . . the finding frogs!"

Finding frogs? Oona liked the ring of that. "What are they finding?"

"Why, all the sparklies that all of us Grands

FUN FAIRY FACT: *Snorgleday is not the only day that is different in a fairy week. Fairies also have Frimpday instead of Wednesday, because who wants to waste all of that time trying to spell Wednesday? Frimpdays are guaranteed to be sunny and warm, with a refreshing breeze and exactly seven puffy white clouds that each look like an animal if you stare long enough. That's why fairies plan all their special events on Frimpdays.*

have lost! I am not the only Grand who tucks things away in safe places that are so safe, I can't find them again. But the frogs have a lot of experience finding fairies from their scolding days. Now they're using that skill for good!"

Oona knew all too well how good the frogs had been at finding fairies when it was time for a scolding. This kind of finding seemed much nicer. "That's great!"

"And the timing couldn't be better," Grandgoop said. "The Unicorn Parade will be coming through any minute, and they love sparklies almost as much as Grands do. Look, we have a whole basketful of gifts!"

"What will the frogs do when they finish finding all your sparklies?" asked Oona. "Because I haven't seen my fairy mittens in a month of Snorgledays, and—"

"You just need to sign up," Grandgoop said, and a magic clipboard and pen appeared in her hand. As Oona signed, she noticed Lucy's name at the top of the list.

"Here they come!" called Grandgoop.

Oona looked up from Lucy's name to see Lucy in real life, her wand held high, leading the procession of unicorns with Molly. At the back of the line of unicorns, Horace and his slugs were busy herding the baby unicorns so they didn't get lost.

The beauty of the unicorns took Oona's breath away, just as it did every year. Their manes and tails were woven with ribbons and gold thread, and their horns shone with an inner light. She reached into Grandgoop's basket and pulled out a sequined scrunchie. Lucy and Molly stopped in front of the Big Banyan Tree, and all the Grand fairies and frogs dropped what they were doing to come out and greet the unicorns.

Oona went up to a silver unicorn and wrapped the scrunchie in its mane. "Welcome home," she whispered.

In return, the unicorn nuzzled Oona's neck. *Thank you,* Oona heard inside her head. *You have shiny hair.* Oona blushed at the compliment.

"Happy quarter birthday!" Lucy said, flitting up to Oona.

Oona blushed even deeper. She couldn't believe Lucy remembered! "Thanks! How's the parade going?"

"Fine as floss." Then Lucy leaned in and whispered, "Molly and I are getting along, don't worry. She's actually pretty funny. She does a hilarious impression of a scolding frog."

"Speaking of frogs, I saw you on the sign-up sheet. What are you using the finding frogs for?"

Lucy looked at her shoes. "It's a little embarrassing."

"I won't laugh, I promise," Oona said, putting on an oh-so-serious face.

"I need them to help me find teeth."

Oona was confused. "From under children's pillows?"

FUN UNICORN FACT: *Unicorns are passionate about hair. They spend almost as much time in the unicorn salon as fairies spend at the dentist. They like their tails and manes curled, permed, or braided, with lots of accessories. If a unicorn comments on your hair, that is a great honor. But be sure to avoid any unicorn having a bad hair day.*

"No, the ones I've already brought home." Lucy sighed. "I don't know if you noticed how, before the whole Fairy Binder disaster, I didn't have any free time?"

"Of course I noticed! That's one of the reasons I started spending all my time working on council business—because I could never find you!" Oona looked at the ground. "I had thought maybe you were mad at me."

"Mad at you? Not at all, I was just super stressed out! Apparently, my cutie Thor loves teeth, just like me." Lucy smiled. "But he's been hiding them the way a squirrel buries nuts. I've found them in puddles all over Blackberry Bog, even deep inside the Chocolate Cave!"

"That's why you were at the Chocolate Cave the other day," Oona said. *Was that how Molly's scarcity spell worked?* she thought. *It made Thor hide Lucy's teeth from her?* But Oona would tell Lucy about that another day. Today, Lucy and Molly were getting along too beautifully.

Lucy nodded. "So these finding frogs are just what I need. I'm going to get all the teeth organized and open Blackberry Bog's first tooth museum! I hope you'll help me."

"Of course!" Oona was gushing about what a fairytastic idea a tooth museum was when Molly came up to them.

"We better get moving, Lucy. We've got four more stops on the parade route before Glitter Gulch." Molly still had a smidge of bossy in her, but now it came with a side of soft and squishy.

The Grand fairies and frogs all waved and cheered as the unicorn parade disappeared into the glade, but Oona just stood and smiled. She suddenly felt very peaceful, and she realized she was the only one in her group of friends who didn't have a special job. Today, she was not very important. But she also knew that wouldn't change how Lucy or Horace or Molly or her Grand felt about her, not by one speck of sparkle.

Today, on the day of the Unicorn Reunion, it was enough just to be Oona.

By day, **KATE KORSH** has been a mild-mannered elementary school teacher, an insightful marriage and family therapist, and a cuddly mother of two, with no magic whatsoever. But by night, she has studied the magical world of creative writing. The Oona Bramblegoop's Sideways Magic series is the culmination of her studies. Kate lives in Los Angeles with her husband and the aforementioned cuddle recipients, who now always seem to magically have clean underwear in their drawers.

@korshkate

**MARTA ALTÉS** is the author and illustrator of many books for children, including the Dork Lord series by Mike Johnston and the picture books *My Grandpa* (an Ezra Jack Keats New Illustrator Honor book), *Little Monkey*, and *Five More Minutes*. Originally from Barcelona, she received her MA in children's book illustration at the Cambridge School of Art, and lives in London with her family. Marta hopes for Oona to visit them very soon, because she is notoriously clumsy.

Marta-Altes.com
@martaltes